For
Connie and Christien,
Thomas and Dominic
and Mrs. Murphy
~R.T.

This edition copyright © 2001
Baby's First Book Club®
Bristol, PA 19007
Originally published in Great Britain 2001
by Little Tiger Press, London
an imprint of Magi Publications
Text and Illustrations © 2001 Rory Tyger
Artwork arranged through Advocate
Printed in Belgium • All rights reserved
ISBN 1-58048-231-7

newton

by

Rory Tyger

CREAK, CREAK, CRE-E-EAK

Newton woke up suddenly.
There was a funny noise somewhere in the
room. "Don't be frightened," he told Woffle.
"There's always an explanation for everything."
He gave each of his toys a special cuddle
so they wouldn't be scared.

CREAK, CREAK, CRE-E-EAK

went the noise again.

Newton got out of bed and turned on the light.
He walked across the room . . .

"See, toys," he said. "There's nothing to be frightened of. It's only the closet door!"

Newton went back to bed again.

FLAP! FLAP! FLAP!
What was that? Was it a ghost?

Once more Newton got out of bed. He wasn't really scared, but he took his bravest toy, Snappy, just in case. He tiptoed, very quietly, toward the noise.

FLAP! FLAP! FLAP!

it went again. "Of course!" said Newton . . .

"Just what I thought."
It was his bedroom curtains,
flapping in the breeze.
"I'll take care of this,"
said Newton.

"You were very brave,
Snappy," he said, as
he closed the window.

SPLISH!

SPLASH!

SPLISH!

Another noise!

Newton looked outside. It wasn't raining.
Besides, the noise wasn't coming from
outside.

Nor was it coming from his bedroom. What was it? "Stay right there, you two," said Newton, "while I look around."

He wasn't the tiniest bit afraid. He was just taking Snappy with him for company.

Newton crept down the hallway. It was
very spooky, especially in the dark corners.

SPLISH! SPLASH! SPLISH!
went the noise.

Very, very quietly, Newton
opened the bathroom door . . .

"Of course, we knew it was the bathroom
faucet, didn't we, Snappy," said Newton.

Newton turned off the faucet, and
tiptoed back down the hallway.
"Shh," he said to Snappy, just
in case *something* in the dark
corners sprang out at them.

Before he got into bed,
Newton pulled back the
curtains - just to check. It
was very, very quiet outside.
"No more funny noises,"
said Newton.

"You can go to sleep
now," he told all his toys.

RUMBLE! RUMBLE! RUMBLE!

"Oh no!" cried Newton. "What's that?"

Newton listened very hard. Not a sound. He was just beginning to think he hadn't heard anything at all when

RUMBLE! RUMBLE! RUMBLE!

There it was again!

Newton looked under his bed.
Nothing there at all - except for an
old candy he'd forgotten about.
"Don't worry," said Newton. "We'll
soon find out what it is."

RUMBLE!
Newton stood
very still.

RUMBLE!
Newton listened
very hard.

RUMBLE! went the noise.
And suddenly Newton knew
exactly what it was!

Newton padded downstairs, and into the kitchen. He helped himself to a large glass of milk and two thick slices of bread and honey. And now he could hear no

RUMBLE! RUMBLE! RUMBLE!

at all, because . . .

the rumbling had been
his empty tummy!

Newton went upstairs again, and told his toys
about his rumbling tummy.
"There's always an explanation for everything,"
said Newton, as he climbed back into bed.
"Goodnight, everyone . . .

Sleep tight!"
SNORE, SNORE, SNORE,
went Newton.